# TEN GOOD RULES

## A Counting Book

by
Susan Remick Topek

photographs by
Tod Cohen

KAR-BEN
PUBLISHING

For my growing family —S.R.T.

Karben Publishing, Inc.
A division of Lerner Publishing Group
241 First Avenue North
Minneapolis, MN 55401 U.S.A.
1-800-4-KARBEN

Website address: www.karben.com

Library of Congress Cataloging-in-Publication Data

Topek, Susan Remick.
  Ten good rules : a counting book / by Susan Remick Topek ; Illustrations by Tod Cohen.
      p. cm.
  ISBN-13: 978-0-8225-7293-0 (lib. bdg. : alk. paper)
  ISBN-10: 0-8225-7293-1 (lib. bdg. : alk. paper)
  1.  Ten commandments—Juvenile literature.  I. Cohen, Tod. II. Title.
  BM520.75.T67 2007
  296.3'6—dc22                                                    2005035998

Manufactured in the United States of America
1 2 3 4 5 6 —JR—11 10 09 08 07 06

When the Jewish people left Egypt, Moses led them to a mountain in the desert. Moses climbed the mountain and talked to God. God gave Moses TEN GOOD RULES for the people to follow, so they could live happily together.

I am the one
and only God.

Do not pray to other gods.

Do not say
bad words.

Celebrate
Shabbat.

Love
your mother
and father.

Do not hurt anyone.

Married people
should love
each other.

Do not take anything without asking.

Do not tell lies.

Be happy
with what
you have.

Moses told the people the TEN
GOOD RULES. They listened and
they promised to follow them.

These TEN GOOD RULES are
just as important for us today.